NO READING PRACTICE QUIZ

D1540952

donated by
Hanson 10/95

E
THO   Thompson-Hoffman, Susan
       Delver's danager

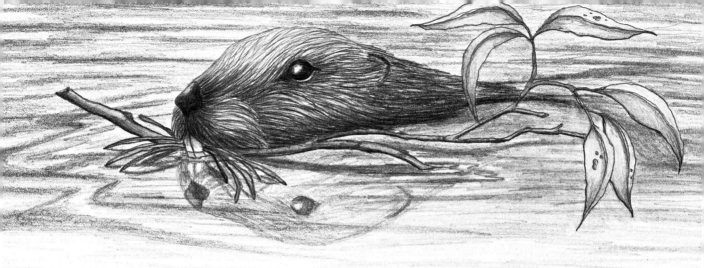

Delver's Danger

by

Susan Thompson-Hoffman

Under the cold moon shining, Delver paddled through the silky water toward his den in the riverbank. Strips of cottonwood and willow bark hung from his mouth like thick whiskers.

The water rippled past the beaver, surrounding his neck and smoothing the fur on his back. Delver listened for the voices of the spirits in the river. Tonight they were peaceful—their voices a gentle murmur. The Colorado River tumbled down, down between the dark walls of the Grand Canyon.

Everything about this night seemed to whisper, "Spring." The willow branches along Bright Angel Creek had begun to turn yellow. Cottonwood buds were fat and ready to burst.

Delver dove deep into the river. He sucked his cheeks closed behind his long front teeth to keep out the water. Clear eyelids slipped down to protect his eyes. He swam to the underwater entrance to his den and dove into the tunnel leading to his home.

When he reached the first dry landing, he rested and let the river water slip off his fur. Then he climbed up to a large, dark room. There his mate Destiny, and their two yearlings waited for him.

Destiny was restless. Soon she would give birth to her babies. Delver added fresh bark to the sleeping pad near her. "Splash and Paddle will be coming back soon," said Delver to comfort her. The two-year-olds were out gathering food. The one-year-olds tumbled and played quietly to while away the time.

Outside, early morning light began to wash over the red canyon walls high above the river. Splash and Paddle hurried to gather their last load of branches. They did not want to remain outside the den in the daylight hours. On the cliffs above the river, their old friend the ringtail watched them as they worked.

Splash pushed his flat tail against the mud. Then he sank his long, sharp teeth into the trunk of a small willow. In five minutes the tree was felled. Paddle cut off some of the tender, upper branches and gathered them in his mouth.

In the den, Delver felt uneasy. Splash and Paddle had not yet returned. Sensing danger, Delver hurried out of the den.

When he surfaced in the river, he spotted Splash and Paddle near the family scent mound. "Everything seems to be fine," Delver murmured to himself as he looked around. Just then the wind changed direction. Now Delver could smell Coyote, close by. Delver looked up. There was Coyote, crouching on a shelf, just above Splash, and ready to pounce.

Immediately Delver slapped his tail against the water with a
deafening clap. Splash looked up, spotted Coyote, and dove
into the rushing river. Coyote lunged, toppling headlong into
the water. "Raaa-ooo-w," Coyote howled in frustration. But
Splash and Paddle were safely gone. High in a safe branch of
a tree, the ringtail chattered with relief, for Orphan had no
love for Coyote.

When Splash and Paddle joined Delver in the den, Delver spoke firmly to them. "You and Paddle have now had a close call with Coyote," Delver said. "You must be more careful. Coyote made an orphan out of the ringtail. Now he wants to make you his dinner. If Coyote can catch a ringtail, he can surely catch you."

"So that is how the ringtail got his name 'Orphan,' " thought Splash.

"Coyote has smelled our scent mound," continued Delver. "The mound helps us by warning other beavers away. But it also endangers us by attracting Coyote. Coyote will move on if he doesn't see us for awhile. Over the next few days, we can stay close to our den and eat the branches we have stored here."

The next morning there was no sign of the beavers on the river. All was ghostly silent. Early morning fog began to slip off the north rim of the canyon. A warm rain fell on the Kaibab Plateau high above the river. All day long heavy rains continued. The snows melted quickly.

Fearful of the prowling coyote, the beaver family stayed close to their den. But high on the north rim of the canyon, way above the river, Tassel, a Kaibab squirrel, was worrying about Delver. Once he had helped Tassel when she most needed help. Now she had a chance to help Delver.

"When warm rains wash over the deep spring snows, there is certain to be a flash flood in the canyon," Tassel fretted. "I have seen it many times." She could see the white water of Bright Angel Creek plunging to the Colorado River below.

That evening, Tassel visited Prickles the porcupine, who lived nearby in the ponderosa pine forest. "Prickles," Tassel said. "The snows are melting too fast. In a day, the Colorado River could rise five feet. We need to get word to Delver that a flash flood may be coming to swamp his den. That will give him time to move his family to high ground."

"Delver's den could be ruined," said Prickles. "Yes you must go and tell him, Tassel."

"I am just about to have my babies," said Tassel. "I cannot leave right now. Could you take the warning to the ringtail, Orphan? He is fast and clever. Of all of us, he can get to Delver the quickest," said Tassel. "You will be safe from Orphan because of your quills, Prickles."

"I CAN'T," said Prickles. "I WON'T. Climbing on canyon walls is your kind of adventure, Tassel, not mine. I like the safety of my ponderosa pine forest. I am fat. I am slow. I CAN'T go."

"Prickles, you MUST. At least, you must try." Tassel was desperate now.

"I am scared," said Prickles, in a small voice.

"Sometimes feeling scared can be exciting," said Tassel. "It's all in how you look at it."

"I will try," said Prickles. She began to walk. She took two timid steps. She stopped. She took one step back. She took two more steps. She hesitated, then took one step back. Soon her feet were moving more quickly. And soon each step was forward, and no step was backward.

Descending the slopes above Bright Angel Creek, Prickles plodded along the redwall overhang. She dillied. She dallied. She trudged and drudged. Then she spotted Orphan under a rock ledge. She brushed against him lightly with her sharp quills.

"Eee-ow!" said the ringtail.

"Sorry, Orphan," said Prickles. "Tassel has sent me to find you. The spring rains are melting the snows on the rim. A flash flood may come. Tassel is afraid the rising water will flood Delver's home. And as Delver is your friend, she thought you would go to Delver as fast as you can, and warn him."

"Of course I will go," said Orphan. "Now that you mention it, I have not seen the beavers for days. I have been a bit worried." And Orphan raced down the trail, leaving Prickles to retrace her steps. She wiggled. She waggled. But this time each step was forward, and no step was backward. She was going home.

Bright Angel Creek roared and tumbled past her on its way to the river below. "Tassel is right," thought Prickles. "This flood is going to be a big one."

Meanwhile, Orphan wove a path among the rocks that no animal but a ringtail could follow. When he had a choice between a slow, safe descent off a steep cliff, or a quick and dangerous leap into midair, he leaped. He stopped now and again to eat insects and lizards, mice and scorpions.

By nightfall, the fearless ringtail reached the river near Delver's den. The beavers were nowhere in sight. Orphan pushed aside the branches of a tamarisk tree that hid the air tunnel leading into Delver's den. Water had already begun to lap against the roots of the tree. "Anybody home?" shouted Orphan, squinting anxiously into the long, dark tunnel. Silence. "Anybody home?" Orphan waited again.

Finally, Delver poked his head out of the air tunnel. "Are you OK?" asked Orphan.

"Yes," said Delver. "We've been holed up because Coyote was lurking around the riverbank."

"He's gone now. Gone downriver, hungry and bad-tempered," said Orphan.

"Well, that is one danger past!" exclaimed Delver. "But I sense more trouble coming. The voices of the river spirits have been loud and demanding for days. Listen. The water is roaring and rushing and the river is rising fast."

"That's why I have come, Delver," said Orphan. "Tassel has sent a warning down from the rim. The heavy spring snows are melting too fast under this warm rain. She fears that a flash flood is coming. She is afraid that your den will be swamped."

Just then Splash appeared behind Delver in the air hole. "Hurry, Dad," said Splash. "The babies are being born!"

"Orphan, I must go," said Delver. "Destiny needs me right now. But thank you for coming with Tassel's warning. Now we may have a chance to survive this flood."

When Delver reached Destiny, three little newborn kits stared up at him with round faces. Delver beamed at them. "When we have taken care of the babies, we will prepare for a flash flood," thought Delver.

There was much to do. First the wriggling babies were licked clean. Destiny combed their fur with her split nails. Then, while they cuddled close to their mother, Delver and Destiny spoke quietly. Paddle and Splash moved closer to hear their words.

"That was Orphan who came to the den, Destiny. A flash flood may be coming. A driving rain is melting the snow on the rim. Bright Angel Creek is already overflowing its banks."

"What will we do, Delver?" asked Destiny. "Our new babies will be too buoyant to swim or dive for several days. They will bob in the water and be tossed against the rocks."

"You and the babies must stay in here," said Delver. He turned toward a dripping sound. Water had begun to trickle through the air tunnel. "Splash and Paddle, you take the one-year-olds to high ground. Stay there until I come to get you. I will dig a new air tunnel that is higher above the river." The older kits nodded in agreement.

Destiny and Delver moved the newborns to the highest corner of the den. Water was rising in the chamber from the underwater passageway. It continued to wash in from the air tunnel. The higher the river rose outside, the higher the water rose in the small room.

Splash and Paddle hurried through the air tunnel, with the two one-year-olds behind them. At last they climbed onto dry shore. Splash and Paddle comforted the one-year-olds. Minutes passed like days. Splash watched the river climb the bank inch by inch. When it covered the air hole entirely, Splash could wait no more. "Paddle," he said, "Take care of the one-year-olds. I'm going back to see if I can help."

Splash took a deep breath and dove down in search of the air tunnel that led to his den. The current pushed him through the long tube. Splash was suddenly afraid. He wondered if he would ever see daylight again.

And then, "thump." He surfaced inside his den, hitting his head on the ceiling. The water had almost totally filled what had once been a dry, cozy bedroom. Splash was floating at the top of the room.

"Thank goodness you came back," said Delver. "The river is rising faster than I can dig. I am not nearly finished with the new tunnel. And we have to break through soon, or we will not have any air in this den."

Delver pointed to where he had been digging a new air passage. "You swim out through the old tunnel, Splash. Begin to dig from the outside," said Delver. "I will stay here and dig. Dig toward my voice until our two tunnels meet."

Destiny paddled to keep part of her body above water. The babies clung to her back.

As the water rose, father and son dug from either side. Destiny comforted the little ones by singing a song:

Sleep little babies, sleep
Sleep little babies, sleep
Swim in your dreams through the waters deep
Sleep little babies, sleep

Delver frantically dug. Splash dug too. Finally, clods of mud gave way and father and son grunted in triumph. Sweet spring air rushed through the tunnel.

With a cry of relief, Destiny crawled up onto dry ground with her three little babies clinging to her back. "We will be safe here until the water goes down," Delver said. Then he turned to Splash. "Now, let's go find Paddle and the kits."

That night, after everyone was fed and huddled close in the new air tunnel, Delver began to speak. "I've never felt prouder of my family than today." He turned to Destiny. "You are so brave, Destiny. You brought us three new babies. Then you trod water for hours, supporting them on your back. You saved their lives."

"But Delver, you deserve the praise," said Destiny. "You never lost your head. Because of you, we weren't drowned in our den."

Delver looked at his family with his dark shining eyes. "It took the whole family, working together, to survive this danger. When the yearlings needed protection, Paddle was there. When I needed help with the tunnel, Splash returned to finish it with me."

Delver looked lovingly at his two older sons. "You are both two years old now. You are no longer children. Soon, you will leave us to find your own mates. You will dig your own dens and raise your own families." The words of Delver seemed to echo in the den. This was a moment none of the beavers would forget. Then Delver called them to sleep for it had been a long day.

Splash and Paddle stayed with their family until the old den was enlarged and dug higher in the bank. Orphan often came to watch them work. He had long ago passed the word to Tassel and Prickles that Delver and his family were safe.

Then one night, under the warm moon shining, Splash and Paddle said goodbye one by one to their family in the old den. They dove deep into the river that would forever be their home. Delver followed them out of the den. He watched as first one son, and then the other surfaced on the river. He remembered the day, long ago, when he had set out on his own. The river tumbled and turned around his sons as they left. The river spirits sang a gentle song of parting. Delver watched his sons until they rounded the bend in the river, and then they were gone.

To my daughter, Savannah

The author gratefully acknowledges the technical assistance of naturalists George Ruffner of Prescott, Arizona and Robert B. Spicer, of Phoenix, Arizona, Dr. Charles Handley of The Smithsonian Institution, and of her editor, Randy Houk.

Points of Interest in This Book

p. 1.   narrowleaf cottonwood, willow bark
pp. 4, 5.   blue yucca, ringtail, tamarisk tree
pp. 6, 7.   scent mound, coyote
pp. 10, 11. ponderosa pine, tassel-eared squirrel, geese
pp. 12, 13. porcupine, ponderosa forest
pp. 20, 21. cross section of beaver den, Dolly Varden Trout

Text copyright © 1989 by Soundprints Corporation and The Smithsonian Institution. Illustrations copyright © 1989 by Soundprints Corporation, a subsidiary of Trudy Corporation, 165 Water Street, Norwalk, CT 06856.
10 9 8 7 6 5 4 3 2

Library of Congress Cataloging-in-Publications Data
Thompson-Hoffman, Susan   Delver's Danger
Summary: A bank beaver, dwelling in the bank of the Colorado River in the Grand Canyon, enlists the cooperation of every member of the beaver clan to protect the family and the newborns from a flood.
1.   Beavers—juvenile literature   [1.   Beavers]
1.   Thompson-Hoffman, Susan.   11.   Title.
ISBN: 0-924483-02-4

Printed in Singapore